Anna Wilson lives in a village in Northamptonshire with her husband, her two children and two black cats called Ink and Jet. She has written two picture books and plans many more books in the

series.

Nicola Slater lives in the north of England with Dave the cat. Her work can be seen on books and tablecloths around the globe.

Look out for the other books in the

Nina Fairy Ballerina series

New Girl

Daisy Shoes

Show Time

Coming soon

Flying Colours

Double Trouble

Compiled by Anna Wilson

Princess Stories

Fairy Stories

Nina
Fairy Ballerina

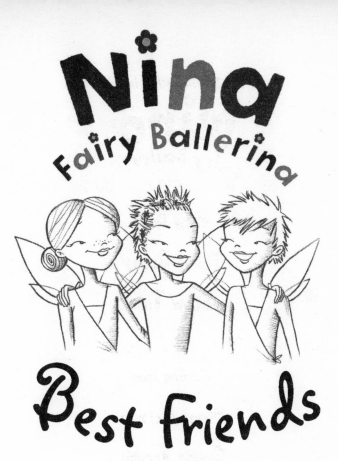

Best Friends

Anna Wilson

Illustrated by Nicola Slater

MACMILLAN CHILDREN'S BOOKS

First published 2006 by Macmillan Children's Books
a division of Macmillan Publishers Limited
20 New Wharf Road, London N1 9RR
Basingstoke and Oxford
www.panmacmillan.com

Associated companies throughout the world

ISBN-13: 978-0-330-43987-9
ISBN-10: 0-330-43987-1

Text copyright © Anna Wilson 2006
Illustrations copyright © Nicola Slater 2006

The right of Anna Wilson and Nicola Slater to be identified as the author
and illustrator of this book has been asserted by them in accordance
with the Copyright, Designs and Patents Act 1988.

1 3 5 7 9 8 6 4 2

A CIP catalogue record for this book is available from
the British Library.

Typeset by Nigel Hazle
Printed and bound in Great Britain by Mackays of Chatham plc, Kent

For Grandma with much love

Chapter One

"**N**ow *that's* what I call a good start to the day," Peri said, sitting back and rubbing her tummy contentedly.

Peri and Nina had just finished breakfast in the Refectory and the first bluebell hadn't yet announced morning lessons.

"Yes, it's nice not to be late for once," Nina said.

"I didn't mean that!" Peri laughed. "You're so sensible, Nina. I meant that honey muffins and hot chamomile tea make a good start to the day."

"Oh," Nina said quietly. Peri had made quite a few comments recently about how sensible and serious Nina was.

Perhaps she thinks I'm boring, Nina thought sadly as she picked up her ballet bag.

The two fairy friends were about to fly to the ballet studio for lessons when Tansy Mugwort fluttered into the Refectory.

"Hey, everyone, listen up!" she cried excitedly. "I've just heard some fantastic news."

"What is it?" asked Peri. Tansy was always the first with a bit of juicy gossip. This had got her into trouble in the past, so she was a bit more careful now about the kind of information she passed on.

"You'll never guess – the Jazz Dance School is sending one of its pupils here for a visit! She'll have to stay in one of our rooms – oh, please let it be mine!" Tansy cried breathlessly.

"Cool!" said Peri.

"Everyone's got to come to the Grand Hall now for a special assembly," Tansy continued. "Madame Dupré wants to tell us all about it."

"Come on, Nina," shouted Peri, grabbing her friend's hand. "What are we waiting for?"

The Grand Hall was already a flurry of flapping fairy ballerinas. "My tummy's rumbling," grumbled Nyssa Bean. "The alarm on my dandelion clock didn't go off this morning."

"Shh! Madame's got some exciting news," Peri whispered. "Here, take these sunflower seeds."

"Thanks," Nyssa whispered back, shovelling the seeds into her mouth.

"Quiet, fairies!" called out the

headmistress. "As you may already have heard, we are expecting a special visitor this week. I have been contacted by Mrs Snapdragon, the headmistress of the Jazz Dance School . . ."

A titter of excitement went up from the fairy ballerinas in the hall. Madame Dupré waited until the noise had died down and then continued.

". . . and I am very pleased to announce that we have arranged for one of their star pupils to come to our Academy for a visit. Mrs Snapdragon and I agree that you will learn a lot from each other. And who knows?" – the headmistress smiled fondly at her pupils – "If this visit goes smoothly, perhaps one of you will be invited to stay at the Jazz School in return. Now, I am relying on you to be sensible and kind to our visitor. We are going to ask a couple of you to share a room with the guest and I think that the only fair way to

decide is to ask my wand to choose the
lucky pair."

Madame Dupré let her wand fall from
her hand and cried out:

> *Magic wand, be fair, be true,*
> *Write clearly in the air.*
> *Spell out the fairy names of those*
> *Who will be asked to share.*

Immediately pink and lavender sparks
flew around the room. Not a fairy stirred
as the wand began to spell out the
names:

Nina Dewdrop
&
Peri Moonshine

"Hey! That's us!" Peri cried, leaping up and punching the air. "Fantastic!"

"You'll have to keep the room tidier then," muttered Nina, still smarting from Peri's earlier comment about her being too sensible.

"I didn't want to share anyway," Tansy said, sniffing. "Our room's already cluttered with all Angelica's shoes."

Peri couldn't help sticking her tongue out at Tansy and grinning at the fact that she and Nina had got one over on Angelica and Tansy yet again.

Madame Dupré was now talking about the fairy visitor.

"Shh – listen!" Nina said, digging Peri in the ribs.

"Nina and Periwinkle, your guest is called Bella Glove," said Madame Dupré.

"Bella Glove!" said Peri ecstatically, her emerald eyes shining. "I bet she's Foxy Glove's daughter – she's the best jazz dancer *ever*."

"And *I* bet we could still teach her a thing or two," grumbled Nina.

"Oh, stop moaning – this is going to be fun," Peri said, hugging her friend.

But Nina brushed her off roughly. "I thought we were supposed to be best friends, Peri?" she said on the verge of tears. "I guess you and Bella will be made for each other. She's sure to be less boring and sensible than I am."

And she flew down the corridor, sobbing.

Chapter Two

Peri stood staring after Nina, her wings drooping.

"What's up, Peri?" asked Nyssa, flying over.

"It's Nina," Peri answered. "I think I've upset her. I didn't mean to . . ."

"Don't worry, Peri. She'll cheer up when Bella arrives."

Peri perked up at the chance to chat more about the visitor and was soon fluttering alongside Nyssa, Nina's mood forgotten.

Miss Tremula, their ballet teacher, was waiting to start the class.

"Has anyone seen Nina this morning?" she asked in her quiet, shaky voice.

"We thought she'd gone on ahead of us, miss," Peri answered anxiously.

"Well, go and look for her, Peri, could you?" Miss Tremula asked. "We've got a lot to get through this morning before Bella Glove arrives."

Peri nodded and was just about to fly down the corridor when a red-eyed Nina appeared. She shuffled into the studio, sniffing and looking at her feet.

"Ah! There you are, Nina, dear," said Miss Tremula.

Nina soon stopped her sulking as the warm-up exercises got under way. She was never happier than when she was chasséing around the studio.

"Now that you are all nicely warmed up, let us continue our work on *Petrushka*," said Miss Tremula. "After all,

Bella is coming to learn about classical fairy-ballet, and who better to show her than you, dears?" She smiled and ordered the excitable fairies to listen as Mrs Wisteria struck up a few bars from the beginning of the ballet.

Petrushka was set in snowy Russia. There was a cruel character called the Showman. He had three puppets called the Ballerina, the Moor and Petrushka the clown.

"Picture the scene, fairies," Miss Tremula commanded. "You are in a crowded marketplace. It is snowing and the ground is icy cold. Crowds are milling around you—"

CRASH! Miss Tremula was interrupted by Peri, who had been imagining herself as an ice sculpture. She had tried to keep still while doing a retiré, which involved standing on her left leg while pointing her right foot into her left knee.

"Hmm, not quite my interpretation of 'graceful'," said Miss Tremula pointedly.

Peri blushed and shook out her crumpled wings.

Once the class had listened to more of the music, they divided up into small groups to work out a routine. Nina and Peri were soon squabbling over who was to be the Showman playing his flute and who the Ballerina. Of course, they both wanted to be the Ballerina.

"You always give yourself the best parts, Nina," Peri grumbled. "I want to have a go at being in the limelight for a change."

"Well, perhaps you could be Petrushka, then," Nina said angrily. "You're good at making a clown of yourself, after all."

"Stop it!" cried Nyssa. She had never seen Nina and Peri argue like this.

"What's all the fuss, fairies?" asked Miss Tremula. "Calm down, Peri. There's

no need to get your wings in a twist. I'm sure we can sort this out."

"No, we can't!" shouted Nina. "Per—"

BANG! Nina stopped short at the sound of the studio door swinging violently shut.

"Hey, guys!" A tall, slim fairy stood in the doorway with her hands on her hips. She had short elfin-style black hair pinned back from her face with clusters of glimmering hairclips. She was wearing a green leotard with a silver leaf pattern embroidered on it. Her almond-shaped brown eyes glinted mischievously and she had a broad grin on her face. Her wings were the brightest silver Nina had ever seen.

"I thought you ballerinas were supposed to be dainty and quiet. Looks like you're going to prove me wrong!"

Bella Glove had arrived.

Chapter Three

After a quick lecture from Miss Tremula on how to address the teachers at the Royal Academy of Fairy Ballet, Bella sat quietly on a bench to watch the class.

"She must be bored stiff," said Peri under her breath.

"Why?" Nina asked, shocked at the idea that anyone could find ballet boring.

"Well, just look at her — she's so cool! I bet they don't have to pretend to be clowns and dolls at the Jazz School," Peri said.

Nina just raised her eyebrows and decided not to speak to Peri for the rest of the lesson.

After ballet class, Bella was introduced to Nina and Peri and told that she would be staying in their room.

"It's break time now, so why don't I give you a guided tour?" Peri asked Bella eagerly.

"It's cool, your Miss Meadowsweet met me in the office and showed me around already," Bella said, fiddling with her hairclips. "But hey, Nina, you got a scholarship to this place, right?"

Nina shrugged her shoulders and muttered something under her breath.

"I've always wanted to know more about classical ballet," Bella continued, turning to face Nina.

"You have?" Nina said.

"Yeah, of course. That's why I'm

here, isn't it?" Bella answered. "Nina, why don't you show me your room and we can chat on the way?"

"It's my room too!" Peri piped up eagerly. But Nina and Bella were already whizzing off to Charlock corridor, giggling and gossiping.

"You're a fantastic dancer, Nina," said Bella. "I was watching you in class just then."

"No, no, I'm not really," Nina said, blushing furiously.

"Duh! Of course you are! Mrs Snapdragon told us how difficult it is to get a place here, let alone win a scholarship. And you *were* chosen by Magnolia Valentine – that's mega!" said Bella.

"You've heard of Magnolia Valentine?" Nina couldn't believe that this trendy fairy knew the name of a famous prima ballerina.

"Who hasn't? She's the first name that

comes to mind when you think of the fairy corps de ballet," Bella said.

"Sounds to me as if you should be here rather than at the Jazz School. Why aren't you?" Nina asked.

"Oh, it's a long story," said Bella dismissively. "Hey, is this your room?"

The two fairies had arrived at Charlock corridor. Nina was shocked to see how much luggage Bella had brought with her. The school porter fairies had delivered her bags directly to the room, but they had had trouble

finding enough space. The floor was covered with boxes, trunks and bags, and Nina's and Peri's beds were littered with luggage too. The window seat had a special foldaway bed stored in it for visitors, but it hadn't even been pulled out yet – there was simply no room to move.

Nina gasped. "You've got so much stuff! What in all fairyland are we going to do with this lot?"

"Don't worry," Bella reassured her. "I'm useless at packing and always bring too much stuff. A bit of magic will sort it."

"You can't use magic at the Academy," Nina said nervously. "That would be breaking the Number One Fairy Rule."

"No problem – I'm a guest, remember?" Bella said, grinning mischievously. "The rules don't apply to me."

And so saying, she whipped out her wand and, jabbing the air with it, she rapped out:

I'm useless! I'm hopeless!
I have packed too much.
Help me now, magic —
Organize my stuff.
Take away some things
And tell me what to do!
I surely don't need
Every ballet shoe.
I seem to have packed up
My whole collection.
Help me, magic —
Use some wise reflection.

ZAP! WHIZZ! POW! Nina was thrown against a pile of soft cushions and the room was filled with a mist of silver sparks, fizzing and exploding like fireworks. Nina rubbed her eyes — the room now looked as neat as she had left

it that morning. Even Peri's side of the
room was tidy for once.

"That was amazing!" Nina gasped
shakily.

"Check out the wardrobe," said Bella.
"It'll all be sorted now."

"What's going on, guys?" Peri asked,
bursting into the room.

"Bella's just done the
coolest tidying spell!"
Nina said, glowing
with admiration.

"Done what?
But you *hate* it
when I
do magic
in our
room!" Peri
objected.

"Yes, but she's a guest. The rules don't apply to her, do they?" Nina said, looking at Bella proudly.

Peri went over to the silver birch wardrobe and some sparkly dust came off on her hands as she opened the doors. "What's all this glitter?" she asked, brushing it off. "And where have all my things gone? You've taken over my side of the cupboard!" Peri shouted.

"Oh, sorry, Parry," said Bella.

"It's *Peri*, actually," said Peri.

"Oh, right. Well, Peri-actually," said Bella, grinning, "I'm sorry, but I don't have complete control over my tidying spells just yet. I've only just learned them, you see."

"Thanks, Nina, thanks a lot," said Peri, looking very hurt. "So much for all that stuff about best friends." And she fluttered away.

Chapter Four

Peri went and found Nyssa.

"I don't trust that Bella," she said. "I think there's something she's not telling us. And I intend to find out exactly what that is."

"Peri, don't you think you're overreacting a bit?" Nyssa said. "I mean, I know it's not nice when your best friend makes friends with someone else—"

"I'm not jealous!" Peri said, trying to hide her feelings. "I don't want Nina getting hurt by Ms Jazzy Pants, that's all."

✿

Nyssa and Peri hurried off to class. To Peri's disappointment, Bella now had been told to join in.

"Good morning, fairies! Are we *all* listening?" Miss Tremula looked pointedly at Nina and Bella, who were chattering away. "Now, first we are going to focus on our demi-pointe."

"Erm, excuse me!" Mrs Wisteria was trying to get Miss Tremula's attention.

"Yes, Mrs Wisteria?" said the ballet teacher a little impatiently.

"I don't seem to be able to locate the piano." Mrs Wisteria gestured at the empty space in front of her.

"I'm sorry?" Miss Tremula began. "Oh! I see what you mean! Where can it have got to? Pianos don't just disappear."

"Maybe another class has borrowed it?" said Peri, trying to be helpful.

"Of course not, Periwinkle!" said Miss Tremula. "You know very well that each

class has
its own
piano.
Really,
this is most
irregular. I
think this
constitutes
something of an
emergency, so I
will have to use
a little magic.
Let's see now . . ."

Taking up her cane,
which doubled as a
wand, Miss Tremula
closed her eyes.
Concentrating hard,
she waved her wand
in the air. As a
stream of pink
glitter shot out
across the studio,

Miss Tremula sang:

Piano, come back.
Please give us the chance
To learn the steps
Of our new dance!

Nothing happened.

Nina looked anxiously at Peri.

"I don't understand it," Miss Tremula said, looking a little flustered. "My magic's never let me down before."

"Shall I go and see if I can find the piano?" Peri asked helpfully.

"Yes, all right, dear. Ask Miss Meadowsweet in the office if she can help you," said Miss Tremula.

Peri eagerly fluttered out of the ballet studio.

"In the meantime, fairies, we will start our warm-up exercises," continued Miss Tremula, regaining her composure. "I'll conjure up some music."

Miss Tremula tried another spell:

Please help us, fairy magic.
We need a melody —
Something we can dance to
With joy — and happily.

Immediately a raucous cacophony of
screeching bagpipes filled the room,
making it impossible for anyone to hear
themselves think, let alone follow
anything Miss Tremula was trying to
say.

Everyone was shrieking, "Stop!" and putting their hands over their ears. Everyone, that is, except Bella, who didn't seem at all bothered by the rumpus. Eventually the noise faded away.

Miss Tremula was shaking even more than usual. She felt very ashamed that her magic had produced such terrible results and was keen to get her fairy ballerinas back to work at once.

"As I said before, we will work on our demi-pointe today," said Miss Tremula quietly. "If you are to work up to wearing ballet shoes with blocks, you must think about strengthening your feet."

Miss Tremula carefully rested her cane against the mirror and, holding her tutu out delicately, she rose up on tiptoes in her soft lilac ballet shoes. Then she gently lowered herself down again.

"Now it's your turn, fairies," Miss

Tremula said and sat down to watch
them.

The class spent the next few minutes
practising – rising up on to demi-pointe
and returning to a standing position.
Once they had got the hang of this
without wobbling, Miss Tremula asked
them
to skip
around the
ballet studio in
a circle, staying on
demi-pointe.

"Bella – that's
lovely, dear! Look at
Bella, everyone – her
feet are nice and dainty.
She lands as gracefully
as thistledown, whereas
some of you sound more
like mad March hares,
thumping around the
place. Come on –

tummies in, bottoms in, long necks! Beautiful, Bella! Well done, dear!"

Everyone admired the graceful dark-haired little imp as she leaped around the room as light and airy as a leaf carried on the wind. Her silvery leotard glinted as she flew, and her eyes shone.

Suddenly Peri burst into the room, gasping and panting.

"Miss Tremula, Mrs Wisteria – come with me, quickly! I've found the piano!" she cried.

"Oh, well done, Periwinkle," said Miss Tremula, looking very relieved. "But where is it?"

"You'll never believe it," Peri said. "It's flying around the meadow – look out of the window!"

Peri was right – there in the sky, above the field of wild flowers, was the piano, swooping and gliding gently on the breeze like a giant bird.

Chapter Five

"How in the name of enchantment did the piano get up there?" cried Miss Tremula, fluttering her wings irritably. "And why is it covered in that shiny dust?"

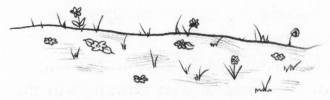

I'm sure I've seen that glitter somewhere before, Peri thought, looking over at Nina and Bella. The two new friends were laughing and pointing up at the piano, just as the rest of the class was. But Peri could have sworn she saw Bella flick her wand quickly behind her back.

All of a sudden the piano stopped gliding above the fairies' heads and gently floated down to the ground.

"Thank goodness," said Miss Tremula. "You're going to have to help me, fairies. I'm not leaving anything to chance – or magic – this time. Let's push it back inside."

With a great fluttering of wings, the First-Year fairies managed to get the piano back to the ballet studio.

Fortunately the rest of the class passed uneventfully. The fairy ballerinas sat in a circle and bent and flexed their toes to warm up the muscles in their feet and legs. Once the class was all quiet and focused again, Miss Tremula showed them how to perform a graceful sauté,

landing softly in first
position.

"That's
beautiful, Nina.
Now, Nyssa,
careful you don't
land with too
much of a
thud. We are
fairy ballerinas,
after all, not toads.
Periwinkle,
please look at
Bella's feet and
try to copy her.
That's right, turn your
toes out nicely for first
position. Remember to
keep breathing,
everyone! I don't want fainting fairies in
my class." Miss Tremula was back into
her stride once more, the magical
mayhem forgotten.

Throughout the class Bella excelled at everything the fairies were asked to do.

Peri's feet followed all the instructions from her ballet teacher, but her mind was elsewhere. What was all that weird magic this morning? she thought. And how come someone who's supposed to be a jazz dancer is so brilliant at ballet? Peri decided she must get to know Bella better.

I know! she thought. I could throw a party for her in our room! That would get her attention. And maybe Nina would remember I exist too.

At break time Peri rushed off and started planning the party. She went down to the Academy kitchens to see what she could lay her hands on. Peri was popular with the cooks and the dinner-fairies, as she was always quick to tell the kitchen staff how much she loved their food.

"I wondered if you could do me a

favour," she said to Basil, the head cook. "You know we've got a visitor called Bella staying with us?"

"Yes – why?" Basil replied.

"Well, I want to give her a proper welcome," said Peri. "She's staying in my room, so I thought we could throw a party there this evening."

"Ye-es?" said Basil, sounding unsure about the idea.

"Well, that's where you come in!" said Peri cheerily. "Could you do us some party food – please?"

"Well, OK, as long as you stay out of my way, young fairy!" said Basil. "I suppose you'd better tell me what's on the menu."

"You're a star!" Peri hugged the cook tightly. Then she drew up a chair and started telling Basil exactly what she had in mind.

Chapter Six

After break Peri arrived back in class out of breath and grinning wildly.

"Listen up, guys!" she called out. "I thought it would be a good idea to give Bella a proper welcome."

The fairy ballerinas all nodded in agreement.

"So," Peri continued, "I've arranged a party in our room on Charlock corridor after lessons this afternoon. You're all invited!"

"That's a great idea, Peri. That's so

kind of you," Nina said, smiling and hugging her friend. Peri blushed. It felt like ages since Nina had been so nice to her.

At the end of class the fairies curtseyed to their teacher and flew down the corridor to get ready for the party. Nina wanted to look her best.

Bella will love my daisy dance shoes! she thought to herself as she got changed. She chose a white sparkly leotard and matching tutu to go with the shoes, and she pulled her hair back with a white and silver hairband.

"Are you ready, Nina? You look great!" Peri said. "Can you come to the kitchens with me?"

The two friends flew to pick up the food that Basil had been busy preparing.

"This looks fantastic, Peri," Nina said, drooling over the plates of fairy cakes and meringues. "How on earth did you get Basil to do all this so quickly?"

"Just my natural fairy charm, I guess!" Peri giggled.

Nina and Peri arrived back at their room to find the door already open. The beds had been pushed into the far corner of the room, all the fairies' clothes and shoes had been neatly tucked away and, most surprising of all, there was a table in the middle of the room laden with delicious-looking treats. There were pumpkin pancakes, chocolate-covered cherries and

sugary marshmallow muffins. There was a huge pile of poppy-seed profiteroles and even some piping hot mugs of steamy, creamy hot chocolate. Strangely, some of the food seemed to have a sprinkling of sparkly dust . . .

"Peri! Why did we go to the kitchens to get all this food if you'd already organized this up here?" Nina asked.

"Er . . . erm . . ." Peri was completely bewildered.

"Hi!" Bella suddenly appeared from behind the door. "I thought I'd better contribute something to the feast too, Peri," she said, smiling.

"Right," Peri said. She quietly set down a tray of meringues. "Thanks, Bella."

Outdone again, she thought miserably.

❋

The party went ahead as planned, with
fairies cramming themselves into every
tiny space available. Some of them ended
up sitting on top of the wardrobe, others
hovered just outside the open window.
The rest spilled out into the corridor.

Peri put on a brave face and made an
effort to enjoy herself. She even found
some jazz in her collection of discs and
played it on her Daisy Discplayer. She
thought it might help to make Bella feel
more at home. And she wanted Nina to
see that she could be friends with both
her *and* Bella.

I'm not going to show Nina how I
feel, Peri thought bravely.

Bella seemed to be having a ball, but
Peri couldn't help noticing that she
changed the jazz music back to ballet
when she thought Peri wasn't looking.

What *is* she up to? Peri wondered.

Chapter Seven

The next morning after breakfast Bella and Nina hurried to the ballet studio for lessons as usual. Peri had not made it to the Refectory with them.

"Where *is* Peri?" Bella asked Nina.

There was no time for chatting, however, as Miss Tremula had arrived.

"We're going to do some more work on *Petrushka* today, dears," she said. She scanned the room. "Oh, Periwinkle doesn't seem to be here yet – well, I'm sure she'll be along in a minute."

Miss Tremula turned to Bella. "How

about giving us a little demonstration while we wait, Bella?" the teacher asked. "Maybe we could learn something from *you* today?"

The class murmured and nodded in agreement. Everyone was keen to see how this intriguing newcomer danced at *her* school. But Bella just shrugged at Miss Tremula and said, "I don't really feel like dancing at all today."

Miss Tremula was rather taken aback. No fairy had ever had the nerve to refuse to dance in her class before. However, Bella was a guest, so Miss Tremula decided she would have to tread very carefully.

"I think it would be good for us to watch you, Bella, dear. After all, one of our fairies might be inspired to go and visit your school in exchange!" the teacher coaxed.

"I said, '*no*'!" Bella said, her brown eyes glinting dangerously.

"Looks like a case of all tutu and no talent!" muttered Nyssa.

"Bella Glove – !" said Miss Tremula angrily. But she didn't have time to finish reprimanding Bella, because the spiky-haired imp had already whizzed out of the studio and down the corridor.

"I'll go and see what's the matter, miss," said Nina anxiously. But just at that moment Peri arrived.

"Sorry I'm late,

Miss T. Have I missed anything?" she asked, trying to get her breath back.

The class giggled.

"You could say that, Periwinkle, yes," said Miss Tremula, smiling. "Our guest has, shall we say, flown off the handle at me."

"Ah, yes . . ." said Peri. "Well, that's why I'm late, actually."

"I think you'd better explain yourself, Periwinkle – I don't understand," said her teacher.

"The thing is, I've been doing a bit of research on Bella Glove – and she's not all she seems," Peri said rather cryptically.

"Yes she is!" Nina cried angrily. "You've just been jealous of her since the moment she arrived."

"Well, yes, I admit I was jealous of the way she flew in and stole my best friend," said Peri cautiously. "But the thing is, it's true Bella is Foxy Glove's daughter, but – and this is the important bit – she's a useless jazz dancer!"

"Peri!" cried Nina, very upset that her new friend was being talked about in this way.

"It's true!" Peri said. "That's why she's here. She's failed miserably at every class, exam and test she's had to do at the Jazz School. She's always wanted to be a classical ballerina, but her mother wouldn't let her. Then the chance of a school exchange came up – Madame Dupré, Queen Camellia and Mrs Snapdragon came up with the idea at the Dance Schools' Conference last year. The Jazz School needed an excuse to get rid of Bella for a bit."

"Well, it would certainly explain why Bella didn't want to show us anything she'd learned at *her* school," said Miss Tremula. "But I don't understand how she can be so bad at jazz when she's done so well in my class here."

Bella stormed back into the studio, her brown eyes blazing. "You just don't get it, do you?" she fumed. "All my life it's been 'Foxy Glove this, Foxy Glove that'. Everyone loves my mother, and they all want me to be just like her. I only got into the Jazz School because of her. And everyone knew it, so no one wanted to be my friend. I decided right from day one that I would flunk everything. I thought if I behaved badly enough, they'd chuck me out. And then I got the chance to come here."

"Oh, Bella, why didn't you tell us this to begin with?" asked Peri.

"I thought you'd all ignore me like they do at the Jazz School," said Bella, tears rolling down her cheeks. "Then when I saw how easy it was to get your attention – just by the odd magic trick and copying a few ballet moves . . ."

"So it was *you* who put a spell on the piano?" said Miss Tremula. "Well, Bella, dear, I don't think that was really necessary or sensible, was it?"

"No, well, when you're Foxy Glove's daughter, you spend your whole life doing things that are 'necessary and sensible'," said Bella sarcastically. "And I've had enough!"

And to Bella's surprise, the whole class cheered!

Chapter Eight

Now that the truth about Bella was out, Peri found her much more friendly.

"You know, Peri, I should thank you really," said Bella the next day.

"Why's that?" said Peri, blushing.

"Well, it was such hard work lying all the time to everyone about my school. At least everyone knows now. And I'm really sorry if I came in between you guys," she added, putting one arm around Peri and one around Nina. "You're both great, and I love sharing a

room with you. Will you forgive me, Peri?"

"Yeah, of course," said Peri.

"Cool! I've never even had one true friend before, let alone two!" said Bella. "Maybe Madame Dupré will let me stay. What do you reckon?"

"Maybe!" said Nina excitedly. Then a sudden thought struck her. "But what about your mum, Bella? You're only supposed to be visiting. What is she going to say if you want to stay?"

"I don't know," Bella admitted. "I'll

cross that bridge when I come to it. Now let's get dancing!"

"We've had a lot of interruptions over the past few days," Miss Tremula said firmly. "Now we really have to concentrate on *Petrushka*. I would like you all to think about the scene where the Showman locks Petrushka and the other puppets away in their cells. This is a very sad, dark part of the ballet and you will need to think hard about your moves."

"I've got an idea, miss!" said Peri enthusiastically. "Why don't the puppets start their dance by sitting on the floor, hugging their knees into themselves – like they are trying to curl up into a little ball?"

"That's good, Peri," said her teacher encouragingly. "Let's try it – everyone sit down, please."

The fairies all got down on to the

wooden studio
floor and copied
Miss Tremula.
They hugged their
knees tightly into
their bodies, but had
to concentrate on
pointing their
toes down neatly
and folding their
arms gracefully
around their knees.

"That's right! Now,
bend your heads
gently down on to
your knees as well – long
necks, please!" Miss Tremula
commanded. "Lovely – you are trying to
make yourselves as small as possible.
And," she continued, "when the
Showman comes to unlock your cells,
you must spring to attention again, like
this."

Miss Tremula gave a demonstration. She curled up into a ball and then shot out her slim legs, straight and strong. Her toes were beautifully pointed and her arms were held above her head with her hands gracefully curved.

"The Showman can see that his puppets are all wide awake now and ready to perform for him," said Miss Tremula. "Now let's see you all do it."

Miss Tremula watched carefully as her ballerinas all repeated this exercise.

"Right, Mrs Wisteria, I think we are ready now. Will you

begin, please?" Miss Tremula asked the pianist.

The dreamy music carried the fairies away to the cold city where the puppets lived with the evil Showman. They pictured themselves there, locked away, sad and lonely.

"Now that you have heard the music, I would like to divide you up into groups of three. Work hard, fairies – I am going to ask the best trio to perform to the rest of the class. Now, Nina and Peri, I think you should dance with Bella . . ."

Nina was the Ballerina, Peri was Petrushka and Bella was the Moor. "After all," Bella said, "in the ballet, the Moor tries to capture the Ballerina's heart and makes poor Petrushka jealous. A bit like me with you two, I guess," she added quietly.

"I think the clown should do a clumsy dance – what about doing spring points like this?" Peri suggested. She stood in

first position, her toes turned out, and
then pointed her right leg out in front of
her. Then she switched legs, hopping on
to her right leg and pointing out her left
leg.

Miss Tremula
came over to
see how the
trio were
getting on.

"That's
lovely, Peri. But
try not to stick
your tongue
out while
you are
doing your
spring points!"

The three
fairies giggled together
and went back to
practising.

"Wouldn't it be

great if we three were chosen?" Nina whispered.

Bella was just about to agree wholeheartedly when the colour drained out of her face. "Somehow I don't think that's going to happen," she whispered back.

"What's the matter, Bella? You look awful!" said Peri anxiously.

"I'll tell you what the matter is!" boomed a stern voice from the open doorway. "I've just had your school report, young fairy!"

"Mum!" Bella gulped.

"Foxy Glove!" gasped Peri.

Chapter Nine

Bella had been dragged out of the studio by her mother – a very stern-looking fairy with long dark hair and almond-shaped eyes just like Bella's.

Mother and daughter were now inside the headmistress's office

"So you call yourself a headmistress?" Foxy sneered. "If you knew what kind of a dancer my daughter was you'd never have invited her to the Academy. Have you seen her awful school report?"

"Why don't you go and make us all a nice cup of chamomile tea, Bella?" Madame Dupré suggested.

Bella meekly left the room.

Once she had gone, Madame Dupré turned to face Foxy. The headmistress made herself look as formidable as possible.

"I'm sorry to hear that you are so disappointed with Bella," she said. "I think you will find that your daughter has every chance of becoming a very gifted fairy ballerina."

"But I don't want her to be a classical ballerina!" Foxy shrieked. "No one in the entire history of the Glove family has ever been a classical ballerina!"

"There is a first time for everything, and I can assure you that it is what your daughter wants," Madame Dupré replied soothingly. "May I suggest that you come and watch her dance this afternoon before you make any rash decisions?"

Foxy Glove reluctantly agreed and took the cup of chamomile tea that Bella was offering her. Bella then gave Madame Dupré a huge grin and rushed off to tell Nina and Peri the good news.

"Madame Dupré has made Mum give me a second chance!" Bella told her friends.

They were flittering over the wildflower meadow outside the Academy.

"Oh, I wish she'd let me stay here with you guys instead of going back to that toad-hole of a place . . ."

"Well, let's make that wish come true then," Peri suggested.

"Yeah, like that's really easy," Bella said sarcastically.

"If you can make pianos fly, surely

you can make wishes come true?" said Nina, laughing.

"No, that's the thing. I have never had a wish come true," said Bella sadly.

"That's where your friends come in," Peri reassured her. "Didn't you know that the number three has always been a special, magical number?"

"So?" said Bella, raising one eyebrow.

"Well, there are three of us, aren't there?" said Peri. "You know the saying 'Two heads are better than one'?" she continued.

"Yes, yes – so what are you saying?" asked Bella.

"Well, in fairy magic, three heads are better than two! If we hold hands and make a fairy ring, we can wish our wishes together and they are bound to come true," Peri explained. "That's what my granny always told me anyway. I've never tried it before, but now is as good a time as any, isn't it?"

"May as well give it a go," said Nina. "Come on, Bella – what have you got to lose?"

"Not a lot!" Bella agreed. "OK – what do we have to do?"

"Right, hold hands," Peri said. "Now, dance round slowly and quietly and say your wish in your head – do *not* say it out loud, whatever you do."

Round and round the fairy friends

danced, quietly repeating their special wishes in their heads. Peri wished over and over again that Bella could stay and that she and Nina would be her best friends. Nina also wished that Bella could stay and that all three of them would be chosen to dance for Foxy to show what a great team they were.

Both friends already knew what Bella was wishing.

Chapter Ten

Foxy Glove had agreed to stay at the Academy for the rest of the day and be shown around by one of the Second Years. Tansy Mugwort was chosen for the job and could not believe her luck.

"Ms Glove, I have always been such a big fan of yours! You were so fabulous in *Wild Wish Story*. Mum's taken me to loads of your performances! Can I have your autograph?" she babbled.

Tansy kept up a monologue of praise and adoration for the dancer throughout their tour. Foxy never could resist flattery from a fan, so she was all smiles by the time she reached Miss Tremula's studio.

Madame Dupré was there to greet her.

"Ah, Ms Glove," she said warmly. "I hope that you have enjoyed your tour of the Academy."

"Yes, wonderful," said Foxy. "It certainly is in a beautiful setting – and the facilities are tremendous."

Bella looked at Nina and Peri and raised her eyebrows. She couldn't believe her mother was not bellowing at everyone.

"Well, please take a seat and rest your wings a while. I would like you to see the dance that your daughter has prepared with her friends, Nina Dewdrop and Periwinkle Moonshine. Nina is our scholarship fairy, and is already a very accomplished and talented ballerina. Periwinkle shows great promise as a dancer too," the headmistress added kindly. "Now, fairies, show us the work you have been doing on *Petrushka*."

Nina smiled to herself. Well, that's one wish granted anyway, she thought. Let's hope we impress Foxy.

The three fairies took their places on the floor. Peri did a wonderful dance as Petrushka, using her spring-point sequence to great effect. Nina then showed how the graceful Ballerina was haughty and unkind to Petrushka as she danced for the Moor.

And then Bella came into the scene as the proud Moor – she danced teasingly in front of Petrushka as if to say, "You will never have my beautiful Ballerina."

The dance was so captivating that the whole

studio burst into a round of applause when the three fairies had finished. Even Foxy Glove stood up and clapped her hands.

"I think you will agree, Ms Glove, that your daughter has natural grace and talent," said Madame Dupré.

"Yes," Foxy agreed reluctantly. "I can see that you really are at home here, Bella."

Bella gulped and crossed her fingers tightly behind her back.

"It would be an honour to offer Bella a place here at the Academy," Madame Dupré continued.

Foxy looked at her daughter. "Is this really what you want, Bella?" she asked.

Bella could hardly get the words out, she was so overwhelmed.

"Oh yes – please, Mum!" she whispered.

Nina and Peri cheered and threw their arms around their friend. Another wish granted, thought Nina happily.

"I have some more exciting news to tell you all," said Madame Dupré when the noise had died down. "We found out today that we have an amazing opportunity coming up in a couple of months. Would you like to tell the class, Miss Tremula?"

The old teacher leaned forward on her cane and smiled at her pupils.

"Thank you, Madame Dupré. Yes, fairies: the patron of this Academy, Queen Camellia, has issued an invitation to you First Years to go and perform at the Royal Fairy Palace at the end of next term!" she said, beaming.

The fairy ballerinas gasped and started gossiping away excitedly among themselves.

"Shh! Please, fairies!" said Miss Tremula, holding up her cane to quieten the class. "That is not all – she wants the Academy to be involved at every level. We are to provide all the decorations for the ballet. There will be a huge party afterwards and we need to help organize that too. So Her Royal Fairyness wants three willing fairies to discuss the arrangements with her."

The level of chatter and whirring of wings was building with every word Miss Tremula uttered.

"I don't know about you, Madame Dupré," Miss Tremula added, "but I have a fair idea who we should send to the palace."

Madame Dupré smiled. "I think it would have to be our talented threesome," she said, nodding at Nina, Peri and Bella.

The three fairy friends could hardly believe their ears.

"Well, Bella," said Nina, grinning, "whoever said that wishes don't come true?"

Now read

Nina Dewdrop and her two best friends have been asked to organize a ballet show – at Queen Camellia's Fairy Palace! They must set the stage, choose the decorations for the after-show party and practise their parts.

But when magical mayhem disrupts rehearsals, Nina's sure someone is sabotaging the show. Will it be all right on the fairies' big night?

The fourth funny and magical adventure about Nina and her fairy-ballerina friends!

Log on to

Nina
Fairy Ballerina
.com

for magical games, activities and fun!

Experience the magical world of Nina and her friends at the Royal Academy of Fairy Ballet. There are games to play, fun activities to make or do, plus you can learn more about the Nina Fairy Ballerina books!

Log on to **www.ninafairyballerina.com** now!

Collect three tokens and get this gorgeous Nina Fairy Ballerina ballet bag!

There's a token at the back of each Nina Fairy Ballerina book
- collect three tokens, and you can get your very own,
totally FREE Nina Fairy Ballerina ballet bag.

Send your three tokens, along with your name, address and
parent/guardian's signature
(you must get your parent/guardian's permission to take part in this offer)
to: Nina Fairy Ballerina Ballet Bag Offer, Marketing Department,
Macmillan Children's Books, 20 New Wharf Road, London N1 9RR

Nina Fairy Ballerina
Bag Offer

1 Token

Collect 3 tokens and get your free ballet bag!
Valid until 31/12/06

A selected list of titles available from Macmillan Children's Books

The prices shown below are correct at the time of going to press. However, Macmillan Publishers reserves the right to show new retail prices on covers which may differ from those previously advertised.

Anna Wilson

Nina Fairy Ballerina New Girl	0 330 43985 5	£3.99
Nina Fairy Ballerina Daisy Shoes	0 330 43986 3	£3.99
Nina Fairy Ballerina Best Friends	0 330 43987 1	£3.99
Nina Fairy Ballerina Show Time	0 330 43988 X	£3.99

All Pan Macmillan titles can be ordered from our website, www.panmacmillan.com, or from your local bookshop and are also available by post from:

Bookpost, PO Box 29, Douglas, Isle of Man IM99 1BQ
Credit cards accepted. For details:
Telephone: 01624 677237
Fax: 01624 670923
Email: bookshop@enterprise.net
www.bookpost.co.uk

Free postage and packing in the United Kingdom